Linda was my girlfriend. She was a right laugh.
'How do you make an apple puff?' I didn't have a
clue. Her jokes were always pretty daft. 'You chase
it round the room. Oh, and here's another one . . . . '
I was always telling her to give her jokes a rest.
'Listen, this is a good one. There were three nuns
on holiday in a mini . . . . '

Linda was great fun. Some of her jokes were rough,
but talk about a laugh. She always had a funny
story to tell – most of them she made up herself.
You could listen to her for hours. She knew more
jokes than anyone I know. Funny things were always
happening to her and she never forgot about them.
She was so lively.

Some of her puns were old. I'd heard them stacks
of times, but it was the way she told them. She
always laughed at her own jokes. Her laugh was
great. It was a real chuckle. I liked all her jokes
simply because of that giggle.

Once she started the doctor jokes she never stopped.
'Doctor, doctor, I'm feeling rough, I'm all at sea and

I've got dreadful wind. What can you give me?'
'A boat.'
'Doctor, doctor, I keep thinking I'm a billy goat.'
'How long have you felt like this?'
'Ever since I was a kid.'

She used to sing well, too. Why is it that some
people have all the luck? They are good at
everything. She looked great. She could dance, sing
and make you laugh. When we started going out,
they all said I'd picked a winner there.

They were right. She was great fun. I once said to
her, 'Linda, why don't you go on the stage? You'd
be great'. She laughed. She gave that chuckle of
hers. 'I'd love to. Do you know, I'd really love
that.' For once she sounded quite serious. 'It's
what I've always dreamed about. I want to go on
the stage more than anything else. I'd give my right
arm to be rich and famous.' I wish she hadn't said
that. But she did. I remember it so clearly.

That was all some time ago now. Things have
changed. Don't get me wrong. We didn't break up.
We didn't have a row or anything like that. It was
something much worse. I still go to see her
sometimes — but things are very different. There are
no jokes now. There are no songs or dances. There

are no laughs.   Linda was my girlfriend.   She can't
be any more.

2

We met at school. She was in all the school plays.
I'd known her for a long time but we didn't really
get to know each other well until the ice-skating trip.
A teacher at school ran a trip one night to the ice
rink. It was great. There were hundreds of people
there — all skating round and round together. I
soon got the hang of it and only fell over a few
times. I came across Linda lying spread out in a
puddle in the middle of the ice. I helped her up
and took her round. We skated round and round all
evening. I held her hand and that was the start.

She told people I picked her up at the ice rink. She
was dead right! She said we met on the ice and
have been going round with each other ever since!
Her jokes got worse! That was a long time ago now.

We really got on well together. We enjoyed each
other's company. We were more than friends. Linda
was great to be with. I would do anything for her.

Everything has changed. We can't laugh together now.
We can't go out to discos and share our things. She
will never make me laugh again. Linda is different
now.

The strange part is, we were told something might happen — at least in a way. It was hinted at, anyway. I didn't believe it at the time. I didn't believe this would ever happen but we did have a warning. We were warned but somehow we didn't realize. Perhaps this all sounds like a riddle. I'm not putting this very well. It is difficult to explain and even now I don't understand. You see, someone knew that it would happen and it did happen. It has shattered my life. It has wrecked Linda's.

3

Linda's birthday was on a Saturday last year. We planned lots of things. It was a great day. I went round to her house first thing in the morning. She had stacks of cards. The one I sent her was huge. The postman couldn't get it through the letter box. I took her present round. It was in a box covered in smart red and yellow paper. It was a crash helmet.

It was Linda's seventeenth birthday and she had finally got her mo-ped. It was a present from her mum and dad. She had put some money towards it. She had been saving for ages.

We spent the whole day together. It was great fun. Linda spent most of the morning riding up and down the road on her mo-ped. We all had a go — even her mum and dad. We all tried on the new red crash helmet. Linda looked really good on her mo-ped in that red crash helmet. I told her how it looked like a huge cherry on her head. She called it her cherry hat!

We went out in the evening. There was a fun fair nearby that weekend. It was in a large field. We decided to go there before going out for a meal. It was a warm summer evening. We walked to the fair, it didn't take long. We were laughing and joking all the way. It wasn't very dark but all the lights were blazing away. We could smell the hot dogs and onions a long way off. Music was blaring and girls screaming. It was great. The big wheel ground to a halt and the screams stopped. The fair was packed. Crowds of people were pushing and squeezing past us, carrying goldfish in little bags, or pink candy floss and sticky toffee apples. There were shots ringing out from the rifle ranges, heavy machines thundering and hissing, and squeals of delight at the dodgems. We both thought it was fantastic. Of course, Linda wanted to go on everything. We spent a small fortune! But we had a really good time.

We walked round the side-shows. I had a go on the darts game. It took me three turns but I managed to win Linda a huge pink teddy bear. We really laughed about that. I felt quite proud. She was thrilled.

It was just as we were walking arm in arm past a rifle range that Linda stopped. It didn't take her long to make up her mind. I wish she hadn't. She had seen something.

4

There was a tent with a sign outside. A large board showed several photographs. 'How about going in there?' Linda asked. 'Just for a laugh.'

I read the sign: GIPSY LEE – FORTUNE-TELLER. SHE CAN TELL YOU THE MYSTERIES OF THE FUTURE. The photographs showed Gipsy Lee with lots of famous people. Another notice said, 'Some of the people whose fortunes Gipsy Lee has told. She said they would become rich and famous.'

'Go on, I'll pay,' she said. 'I said I wanted to go on the stage. Let's find out if I will. We'll see if I'll be rich and famous.' I wasn't very keen. It was a waste of money as far as I was concerned. 'You don't believe that nonsense, do you?' I said. 'Oh no, course not – but you never know! Come on, let's go in, just for a laugh.' She tugged at my arm.

As we went towards the tent a face looked out from deep inside. A small, black-haired woman with dark eyes and wearing a shawl said to us, 'Cross my palm with silver and I will tell you the secrets of tomorrow.' I had to laugh. She was just like someone out of a film. I didn't think she was a real gipsy. 'I only

want to hear the nice things. Don't tell me anything horrible.' Linda was already halfway inside.
'Of course, my dear. I don't deal in bad news.'

Linda gave her some money and we were inside. It was gloomy in the tent. It was smoky, too. There were candles burning and a strange smell. In the middle of the table shone a crystal ball. There were playing cards and strange pictures hanging up.

I wasn't too keen on this but I thought there was no harm in it. We all sat down and the gipsy began. 'Oh yes, my dear, I can see you are full of life and joy.' She spoke softly to Linda. 'You have fun and a sense of humour.' I was thinking what nonsense all this was. You only had to look at Linda to see she was a bundle of laughs. Of course she was full of life. Her eyes shone with laughter.

I want to blame that gipsy but I suppose it wasn't really her fault. It's just that if it wasn't for her, Linda might have taken a little more care. That could have made all the difference.

5

The fortune-teller carried on saying things about Linda.
'You are fond of animals,' she said. 'You care about
helpless creatures.'

'You're right,' she said. 'That's why I go around with
him!' It was true. Linda was keen on animals but
any fool could tell that. After all, she was sitting
there holding a huge pink teddy bear and her jeans
always had some of her dog's hairs on them.

'You are learning to drive,' the fortune-teller said
next. That wasn't bad. She was quite close with
that one. Mind you, she probably saw Linda's
licence when she had opened her purse. She planned
to take a test on her mo-ped soon. Linda was
impressed. 'What else can you tell me about myself?'
she asked.

'You tell jokes, you can sing and let me see, you
have a birthday sometime soon.'

'You're right. Today, actually.'

The gipsy looked quite pleased with herself. She had

done quite well so far. She peered into the crystal ball on the table. 'Let me look to the future,' she said slowly. 'Let me see your life unfold. Some is not clear. I can't see it all but, yes, there are good times ahead. You will be getting a letter soon. It will be good news. I can see joy. You will be lucky in any tests or exams you take this year so make the most of it. There is money. Yes, you will be getting a lot of money quite soon.'

Linda was getting really excited. 'What about a job? Am I going on the stage?' That was a mistake! Fancy telling her what she wanted to be. That gave too much away.

'I can't quite see it all. It is still misty,' she whispered. 'Will I be rich and famous? That's all I want to know. Will I become rich and famous?'

'Oh yes, dear, of course. I could tell that when I first saw you. There is no doubt about that. You will become rich and famous all right and quite soon at that. There will be great fame and fortune.'

I had to laugh. You had to admire this woman's nerve. It was all so easy. All she had to do was tell people what they wanted to hear and everyone was happy. That way she could get away with

anything. I just sat there while Linda took it all in.
'Rich and famous' was all she wanted to hear.

'I will tell you three more facts. They will all come
true.' The gipsy took some cards from the shelf.
She gave them to Linda to shuffle and after a while
the old woman looked through them carefully. She
seemed to go into a trance. 'Yes, three facts. One
is your job, two is your home and three is a warning.'
Linda pulled a face at the third. We listened and
waited. I must admit I was getting rather bored.

'First, I can tell you that you will be able to spend
most of your life having others do things for you.
You will move into a large new home with a large
garden. Yes, you will be able to rest while others
fuss around you. You will have no worries.' Linda's
face had lit up. 'This sounds magic. A big house
with servants. Just think of it.' The gipsy carried on.

'Secondly, I can tell there will be new life in your
home and great joy. I see five. Yes, five babies
and all will be boys.'

Linda gave a fit of giggles. It made me laugh too.
The thought of Linda being a mother to five bouncing
baby boys was a scream. We really laughed about
that for days. She still believed it all.

'Thirdly, you will travel and see many places. But take care. I see trouble at the border. I don't know where it is, but it looks like an upset at some crossing between two places. There is danger at the barrier.'

'Oh, that's just the customs. It's happened before when I tried to bring some wine back through customs from France. That's not too much to lose sleep over. Besides, if that's all the bad news there is, I won't bother to go abroad. Simple as that. I'll stay at home and everyone will have to come and see me here.'

6

The gipsy turned to me. I can't remember all she said but it was fairly correct, except the bit about games. She thought I was keen on sport. She was wrong there. I suppose she got that idea from the pink teddy bear. She must have guessed I had won it and given it to Linda. 'You are a kind person and care a lot about your girlfriend.' Who was I to argue? She gazed into the crystal ball again and spoke about my job. I would marry and have children. There was a large grey area that she couldn't see. She said it might show a time of upset or crisis but I would live a long healthy life. Next she started on the cards.

'Again, I can tell you three facts. They will all come true in their own time. First, you will receive a phone call of great importance. Secondly, I must warn you to take care. You are going to lose something. It might even be stolen. It could be valuable.' That was a joke. I didn't have anything worth very much. I told her I didn't have much money. 'Don't let that worry you,' she went on. 'That is the third fact. Your girlfriend here will make you rich, too.'

Linda smiled. 'Who will he marry?' I looked at
her and winked. 'He wouldn't be having five boys as
well, would he?' We giggled. 'That I can't see,' the
old woman began, looking rather worried. Her dark
eyes looked troubled. Linda kept on asking her
questions. But she wouldn't give a direct answer.

'You haven't told me if I will have a long and healthy
life yet.' 'No, I can't see clearly,' she answered very
quietly. 'But you will be rich and famous, without a
doubt.' The gipsy took hold of her hands. 'Let me
read your palms.' She looked carefully at both of
Linda's hands. 'Very interesting.' The old woman
was nervous again. Linda looked really pleased. She
was happy. She obviously believed all this nonsense
about being rich and famous. I was getting a bit fed
up with this fortune-telling rubbish. I just did not
believe in it.

'How long will I live, then?' Linda was still enjoying
all this. 'Many years,' the gipsy whispered, 'yes ...
but .... ' She stopped. She wouldn't look at Linda's
face. 'Very interesting,' she said again. She was
looking carefully at both of Linda's hands.

'Go on, what do they say?'

'It's unusual to say the least. One hand says one

thing and the other just stops. It's as though there is a page missing. There will be a big event in your life. Both hands tell me that but . . . . '

'Go on. I only want to hear the good news.'

'Then comes money — plenty of it, and much fame. Everyone will know your name. But this hand says nothing. It is blank. I can't tell you anymore.'

Gipsy Lee looked up at me and stared with those dark troubled eyes. 'That is all. You must go now.' She looked odd, frightened somehow. I felt a bit awkward. Linda didn't seem to notice. She was still grinning. She had heard what she wanted to hear and nothing could change her mind. She would become rich and famous and that was all that mattered.

I didn't realize it then but that old woman knew something else. It was the way she looked at me and the way she hurried us to the exit. She gripped my arm. 'Take care of her,' she whispered in my ear. I took no notice. I thought it was all part of the act. I was wrong. She must have sensed what was going to happen. I realize that now. Linda's hands revealed a secret all right. It was what her right hand did not show that bothered the gipsy. It all makes sense now.

7

We left the fair ground and went for our meal. It
was a smashing day. We had both enjoyed it a lot.
'I'll remember this day for a long time,' Linda said.
'Thank you for everything. Thank you for all this
and thank you for the present. I shall wear it
always!' It's funny, but I think it was the gipsy who
gave her the best present of all. Linda was so
thrilled after she was told she would become rich.
That had been her dream for years — to become well
known and a success on the stage. She didn't stop
singing that night. There were plenty of jokes, too.
Yes, that fortune teller had actually changed her.
Linda was now much more excited. She was even
happier.

I took no notice of what the gipsy told me. It was
all nonsense as far as I was concerned. We all have
the odd upset or crisis now and again. Why should
one of mine be any different? I was always losing
things and so were most people. It was just rubbish.
I thought no more of it. Linda could not forget her
fortune.

I used to laugh at Linda in her bright red crash
helmet. She took it around with her everywhere.

Once she wore it to a fancy dress party. She wore a long, light-brown dress and that bright red crash helmet. Linda went as a match! Of course she won the prize. She looked great in whatever she wore. There were plenty of jokes about going on strike and being fired! I went wrapped in white paper and was supposed to be a cigarette. Linda told everyone how she was the perfect match for me! It was great fun.

It's funny but Linda began taking silly risks. I noticed how she was not so careful on her mo-ped. Little things made me worried. One day she ran into the road and a car just missed her. I told her to be more careful. 'I don't have to. Anyone who is going to have five children is bound to be safe for a few years yet. Don't you remember those cards? I've only got to be careful going across the border. That's what she told me. All I need to worry about is going abroad. So you see, I'm quite safe whatever I do. With fame and fortune ahead of me nothing can go wrong.' I suppose she had a point.

We didn't see each other for a few days and then suddenly she phoned me up early one morning. She was over the moon about something.

'Do you remember my fortune?' she asked.
'Oh no, what are you on about now?'

'You know – the gipsy. She said I would be getting a letter quite soon, bringing good news. Well it's come! Here it is, I've got it in my hand. It's just arrived!'

She told me about it. She was so sure she was going to be good at singing and acting. Her heart was set on being a star. She had written off to a lot of places and sent them stacks of her photographs. I had one of them blown up really huge and I still keep it on my bedroom wall.

'I told you those pictures would do the trick!' she shouted down the phone. She really was in a good mood. The letter was asking her to do a test at a big theatre. They wanted someone like her to play an important part in a new show.

'This could be the start,' she said. 'One small step for a woman but a giant leap into stardom. You'll see I'll be a star yet. I wouldn't stand a chance normally but that gipsy told me it was a lucky time for tests so I sent off. They want to see me next week. Oh and by the way, my dog is going to have puppies!'

Poor Linda. She was so determined. Her mind was made up. That fortune-teller had made it worse. Linda felt sure that money and fame would come to her because of her talent. She could do nothing wrong now — or so she thought.

That gipsy was right about my upset. It certainly was a crisis. I didn't think I was the sort to cry. It's not really the done thing. I can't help it sometimes. I still feel tears in my eyes when I think of Linda as she was then, on the phone that morning. She was so happy and full of life.

8

Linda had such confidence. She did well on her
mo-ped test. When she came home afterwards, she
tore up the 'L' plates and to celebrate, she painted
bright yellow flowers on the back of the red crash
helmet. It looked really good. On the front she
painted a funny face with a huge grin. There were
two large stickers for eyes. Whenever Linda rode
round on her bike now, no-one could miss her. She
looked a scream chugging up the road with that
helmet on her head!

Linda and I planned to get engaged. I was overjoyed.
'We will have to start saving up,' I said. 'You needn't
worry about money,' Linda said. 'I'll soon be rich.
Don't you remember my fortune? Besides, your cards
told you I'll give you some.' I didn't like Linda
talking like this. She was really sure about her
future. Nothing would change her mind.

'That gipsy has been right so far. She told me I
would be lucky in any tests I take. I passed my test
on the mo-ped without any trouble. My school exams
went well too. I'll pass this test at the theatre as
well. It'll be a piece of cake. You'll see.' I wasn't

so sure. 'I wish you'd forget what the gipsy told you,' I said.

'Why? She's been dead right so far — even with the bit about new life in the home and the patter of tiny feet. There would be five baby boys, remember? The dog had her puppies yesterday. There were five and they're all male! How's that for being spot on?'

She was right, so how could I argue? I said no more but at the same time it made me think. Things could come true but in a very different way from how we expected. That made me worry a bit.

I helped Linda get ready for her stage test. I watched her sing and dance and I tried to give her tips. She didn't need any. She was great. There was no doubt about it, she had stacks of talent. If only she could pass the test. She would get work on the stage and one job would lead to another. This would be a great chance for her. I began to feel as sure as Linda did that she would be a star before long.

The theatre was quite a way from where we lived. Linda decided to take her mo-ped on the train and then ride from the station. 'If I turn up with that helmet on, I'm bound to impress them,' she said with that giggle of hers.

I was more nervous than she was. When the big day came, she rode off to the railway station with a big grin over her face. It matched the one painted on the helmet! She waved and cheered as she chugged up the road. I had to wait for her to phone. She told me she would let me know any news straight away.

'Why are you so nervous?' she said. 'Aren't you forgetting something? You were told. The gipsy read it from your cards. You will be getting a phone call of great importance. Just you wait and see. I feel it in my bones – this will be it. I'll phone you straight after the test. It'll be good news, I promise. I can't fail. I know I'll pass. The gipsy said so.'

What could I say? Linda was so sure. One of those cards had mentioned an important phone call. She was right. It would bring the news we had both been longing for. That's what we thought. All day I waited for the phone to ring.

9

The phone rang early that evening. I had been on edge all day. I had got rather worried. After all, she had been out all day. I thought she would ring much sooner. As soon as the phone rang I darted out to answer it. I was dying to hear the news. I didn't wait to hear her voice, I just giggled down the phone. 'Come on then, Miss Stardom. What's the hold up? I suppose they booked you for the Royal Variety Show ....'

It wasn't Linda. There was a long pause and then a man's voice spoke to me. It was her father on the phone ....

Linda was in hospital. There had been an accident.

'What do you mean? Is it bad?' I asked.

'They don't know. They can't be sure.' Her dad sounded upset. He was in a bad way. I was upset too. This was dreadful. 'What happened?' I asked.

'An accident. Something to do with a train.' This sounded serious.

The next sentence brought me to my knees.

'They think she will lose her right arm.' I was
shocked. I felt so numb. This couldn't happen to
Linda. She was always so lucky. This just couldn't
be true.

It was. I don't really know what I did that evening.
I can't remember it clearly, I was so shocked. I
went to the hospital. The police were there. They
told me what happened to Linda when she was
coming home. I also found out that she had passed
the test at the theatre. She was on her way to a
phone box to let me know. That was when the
accident happened. She must have been so excited.
It happened just before she got to the railway station.

To get to the station, Linda had to cross the railway
line at a level crossing. They said a signal failed and
the flashing light did not work. The gates did not
close so Linda rode over the line. A train was pulling
out of the station and it went right into her. Her
bike was wrecked and dragged along the line. The
police told me about her crash helmet. I felt dreadful.
It had shattered like an egg shell. Linda had been
knocked out and the helmet was in pieces.

'It's foolish what some young people do to crash

helmets,' they said. 'They paint them and put stickers on them and then the helmets are useless. They crack easily. You might just as well wear a paper bag on your head to protect it.' I thought of Linda's helmet with paint and stickers all over it and I felt sick. I felt as if it was my fault.

Linda lay in a hospital bed. She was in intensive care. Her right arm had gone. She had lost a lot of blood. It was touch and go if she would pull through. There could be brain damage.

This was just like a bad dream. It just could not be happening to us. Our future together had seemed so certain. We had made so many plans. Linda had been so happy. What of our future now? Some of what the gipsy told us came back to me. It began to make sense. She had told me to take care of Linda.

She had not been able to read Linda's right hand. It seemed to come to a sudden full stop. Poor Linda. She once said she would give her right arm to be rich and famous. She lost more than an arm. She won't be going on any stage now. She passed her stage test but a few minutes later a train crashed into her. So much for her becoming rich and famous. That was all a lot of lies. That's what I thought at the time, but of course, I was wrong. Linda became very rich and famous — but not in the way any of us had hoped.

10

Linda did not get better. Her brain was damaged. I go to see her but she doesn't seem to know me. Sometimes she smiles and holds my hand but other times she just sits and stares. She can't talk. Not a word. She can manage to sit up in bed but that is all. I even took her dog in for her to see but she did nothing. Her eyes are empty.

I kept one of the puppies. It was Linda's favourite. I still see her parents but they have taken this very badly. So have I. We feel so numb. It happened a long time ago now.

Linda's name and photograph were in all the papers. She was on television, too. You may remember seeing her on The News. People came to my house and I told them everything. They were all interested in Linda. It made headline news: TRAGIC END TO STAR GIRL'S CAREER.

There was a big inquiry. The signals had failed on the level crossing. A big fuss was made to see who had made a mistake. It was even brought up in Parliament. A lot of important people sent Linda 'Get Well' cards — not that they did any good.

After a long time, Linda was awarded thousands of pounds. That made the headlines, too. It was a fortune they paid her.

Linda became rich and famous like the gipsy told her. It happened sooner than we thought. Because of that accident, Linda was given a large sum of money – as damages. But it was no use to her now. The newspapers printed all the details. They were full of it for days. Everyone was interested in Linda's accident. Yes, she had plenty of fame. But it lasted about a week. I was mentioned as well. One newspaper gave her story a headline: THE PRICE TO PAY FOR FAME AND FORTUNE. It is the story I have told you. It is the story of Linda, my girlfriend. She knows nothing about it now. She can't understand.

The police kept her red crash helmet and now show it to people to warn them not to paint or put stickers on any crash helmet. That's how you ruin them. I wish we had known that. It is too late now.

I sometimes go for walks with my dog to the field where the fair ground was. There is nothing there now, of course. I sometimes sit at the spot where the gipsy's tent stood. I remember those cards. They had warned Linda about crossing the barrier – who would have thought that meant at the railway line? They were quite right about other things, too. Linda will now spend the rest of her life having others do things for her. She has already moved into that new large home with the big garden, where she rests while others fuss around her.

I was warned I would lose something. It hadn't bothered me because I didn't believe it and besides, I didn't have anything valuable to lose. I hadn't thought of Linda. There was nothing more valuable than her. She wasn't stolen from me. Stolen things can be replaced or might be found again. Linda was destroyed. She has gone forever. That is the worst part. I see her as she is now and remember how she was. They are two different people. I often think back to her birthday. 'Thank you for everything,' she had said with that giggle of hers. 'I'll remember this day for a long time.'

I suppose I will have to start living my life again. I must try to put all this sorrow behind me. There can't be another Linda. She was special. She had been a right laugh. Linda was more than just a girlfriend. You probably realize that now.